THE SPELL

Roman Garreis

ANAPHORA LITERARY PRESS

QUANAH, TEXAS

ANAPHORA LITERARY PRESS
1108 W 3rd Street
Quanah, TX 79252
https://anaphoraliterary.com

Book design by Anna Faktorovich, Ph.D.

Printed in the United States of America, United Kingdom and in Australia on acid-free paper.

Cover Images: "Sidewall" (1890–1900). Gift of Eleanor and Sarah Hewitt: Smithsonian Design Museum Collection.

Published in 2021 by Anaphora Literary Press

The Spell
Roman Garreis—1st edition.

Library of Congress Control Number: 2021914690

Library Cataloging Information
Garreis, Roman, 1957-, author.
    The spell / Roman Garreis
    56 p. ; 9 in.
    ISBN 979-8-53931-651-8 (softcover : alk. paper)
    ISBN 978-1-68114-557-0 (hardcover : alk. paper)
    ISBN: Kindle (e-book)
1. Fiction—Magical Realism.
2. Body, Mind & Spirit—Witchcraft (see also Religion—Wicca).
3. Fiction—Fantasy—Romance.
PN3311-3503: Literature: Prose fiction
813: American fiction in English

CONTENTS

Blessed Be

Witch of white
Who casts spells from within the energy of light
Where what she sends out it is told
She gets back threefold

Witch of black
Who sometimes cast spells that attack
Not because she truly wants to
But most likely it is what was due

Witch of grey
Balanced in every way
Her intentions are just
But she will cast as she must

Each so magical and pure
Enchanting with such sweet allure
Neither bound by tradition nor decree
Blessed in the ways of old are these witches three

Chapter 1

The Grey Witch

Gabriella burst out her front door and down the steps of her house that sat at 45 Pumping Station Rd in Peabody, MA. She could feel her heart pound as she made her way as fast as she could to the tree line between her house and the Cedar Grove Graveyard. This was finally it, was all she could think about. The day finally was here and she was going to get what she wanted for today was her 16th birthday and as folklore has it at dawn of a girl's 16th birthday was the best chance of finding the witch's house. Finally, she was going to find the witch and get the spell she was seeking for as folklore also had it the witch had the only love spell that would work for sure. It is not like she did not try other love spells but none worked to get the boy of her dreams. In fact, she is a self-proclaimed black witch who tries hard to fit the image with her long dark brown hair, faraway brown eyes, black eye shadow, black lipstick and dark clothes who has often played with black magic spells but has never really been good at it. At best only the love spells worked but all they ever did was get the one she loved to smile at her of which she wanted so much more. But now it all was going to all be different. Now she was going to get a real spell from a real witch which was all she could think about as she broke through the tree line and into the graveyard. Without hesitation she made her way to the unmarked brown tombstone at the northeast tip of the graveyard. This was the spot where folklore says to start from. From there the instructions were clear, face north at the tombstone and walk two miles alongside Fountain Pond then go west into the woods for one mile and there you will find the witch's house in the clearing. Over time so many have tried to find the witch that a path along the pond was created. Over the years it slowly turned into a walkway for all who wanted to stroll along the pond. Gabriella headed out down the path and when she got to where she thought was the two-mile point she stopped. There she found multiple paths leading into the woods created by the many who tried before her. She took a moment to look at them and decided to not take any of them for no one before her was able to say they found the witch. Out the corner of her eye she spotted a very old oak tree that stood out from all of the rest of the trees. This had to be it she thought. This had to be where she should enter as she made her way to the tree. She then placed her back against the tree and headed into the woods. A few yards in a path started to emerge ahead of her. Not one that had been made by others but one that was created naturally. At first, she thought she should not walk it but something inside her told her to just keep moving forward. As she made her way through the woods, she started to realize that she has been walking for hours. *"She should have been there by now"* was all she could think as her anger grew. She just did not understand. How could this be so hard? She knew these woods like the back of her hand. *"Fuck you witch"* she screamed. *"I am not leaving these woods until I get what I came for. You will not make me leave. I will find you. You will give me what I came here for"* she yelled. Gabriella was not one to give up easily. She was raised tough with an embedded meanness and knew how to stand her ground to get what she wanted. She had no doubts that this was where the witch's house was supposed to be. Without her noticing the path narrowed into thick brush slowing her down to almost a stop. But the harder it got the more determined she became as she push through the brush until, suddenly, she broke into a misty clearing. There she could see a little house made of wood with a Grey cat sitting outside the front door. She stood there for a moment gazing at it. *"Could this really be it"* she thought. After a moment she slowly started toward the door but stopped as the cat stood up looked at her and then walked into the house. She then started toward the door again and as she got about half way to the house she could hear a lone crow crowing from a branch of a tall tree off to the right side of the clearing. She glared over at it just in time to see it fly away. This caused her to slightly hesitate as she could hear the crow somehow sounding louder as it faded away into the sky. *"It is just an old crow"* she told herself as she turned her eyes back to the house and continued her way to it. As she reached the house she paused at the open door and tried to look inside. She could not see anything except for the dingy darkness. She could feel her heart pounding again as she could once again feel her anger of how difficult all of this was.   When suddenly a woman's voice echoed from inside the house, *"come in my dear"*. This startled her for a moment but then she stepped through the door and into the house. As she entered the house she stopped right inside the door and looked around. The room was unusually large for what look like a small house from outside. As she looked to the left of her she saw a kitchen that looked more like a root store than a kitchen. Everywhere were jars filled with stuff and things hanging from everything. As she scanned across the room back to the right of her she could see symbols decorating the walls. She always thought that she knew the meanings of all symbols but these were completely different from anything she ever saw. Straight across from her was a huge stone fireplace with a big black pot hanging in it. She became fixated on it for a moment when suddenly from the kitchen she heard the woman's voice again *"hello Gabriella"*. She quickly turned to look to only see the grey cat sitting on the counter with the jars on it. "Here my dear. *Come here so I can get a good look at you,"* she heard from behind her again. When she turned back there was an old grey-haired lady in the rocking chair by the fireplace.

"*Stop fucking with me witch and how do you know my name*" Gabriella shouted.

"*I know you from long ago my dear,*" the old lady said.

"*The fuck you do. I never met you before in my life*"

"*Not from this life my dear. I know everything about you from all lives before this one and I have been expecting you.*"

Gabriella *shrugged it off,* "*Yeah right, then I guess you know what I am here for?*"

"*Yes, I do my dear.*"

"*Then what is it?*"

"*You want the love spell.*"

"*That is right. Can you give it to me?*"

"*Of course, I can but is that really what you want?*"

"*I made my way to here so what do you think?*"

"*You are a young and beautiful girl and really do not need such a spell.*"

"*I really did not come all this way just to hear your opinion witch.*"

"*But my dear you should really listen to my advice. You should not use witchcraft to get love. Love is precious and should be through mutual feelings from within the heart.*"

"*But he feels nothing for me and my heart aches for him.*"

"*Then it is not meant to be.*"

"*Then I will make it be.*"

"*But it will not be real for it will not be from the heart.*"

"*I do not care. I just want him to be with me.*"

"*He will but it will not be with his heart.*"

"*Yes it will. He will love me as I love him. I just need for him to be with me so he will feel it.*"

"*He will never feel it for it will never be real.*"

"*You do not know what you are talking about witch. You are just an old grey haired witch in the woods all by yourself.*"

"*Yes my dear I am what you say but I was also young and foolish in the use of magic and wish to share with you my hard learned lessons.*"

"*Yeah right you learned so much that you ended up alone in the woods. How about you just give me the spell and save the rest for someone else for I really do not need to hear your words of advice.*"

"*Okay if you will not take my advice than heed my warning that a love that is not real is not forever. It is a fake love that has no depth and when a real love comes along it will take it all away from you. This will rip your heart out and shatter your soul leaving you to only feel the depth of emptiness and heartache for as long as you live.*"

"*I will never lose him once I have him so stop with all of your bullshit and give me the spell.*"

"*Okay then here is the spell*" *But, you should reconsider Gabriella; love is not to be played with. People should not be forced or tricked to love. Love is very precious and the most powerful emotion there is. It has the power to make someone the happiest they have ever been within complete bliss while at the same time consume them with utter saddest within ultimate emptiness*" the witch said one last time to Gabriella as she handed her a small piece of paper.

Gabriella grabbed it as fast as she could, stuffed into her pocket and started walking toward the door still disregarding everything the witch had to say. Gabriella turned to tell the witch to just mind her own business but the witch was gone. Gabriella paid no mind and turned and walked out the door. As soon as Gabriella was outside, she headed toward the woods. As she arrived at the edge of the clearing she turned around to take one last look at the house but the house was gone. All that was left there was the Grey cat who was just sitting there staring at her. Gabriella blew it off and turned to enter the woods but found herself back at the graveyard standing in front of the brown tombstone at the stroke of midnight. This did not faze her a bit as she headed to her house with the spell firmly in hand. She didn't even care that the whole day had passed where she spent her whole birthday getting the spell. All she cared about was that she now had the spell. As she made her way back through the tree line and then back into her house where she rushed to her bedroom and for the first time read the spell. The spell read:

1. Fill a glass jar with water.
2. Add 6 red rose petals into a jar.
3. Add 6 rosemary leaves.
4. Add 6 catnip leaves.
5. Add in the blood of a male love dove.
6. Add in a possession of yours that you treasure.
7. Add in the picture of your intended love.
8. Place the covered jar on your altar for 4 days.
9. On the 5th day burn one white and two red candles and uncover the jar letting the smell float freely while chanting 3 times:

> *By the power below and above,*
> *I am asking you to bring me love.*
> *By this spell that I have cast,*
> *I want a love that will always last.*

10. Leave the jar open and the candles burning until the 6th day.
11. On the 6th day the spell will be cast.
12. After the spell is cast recover the jar and bury it in the earth by the roots of an old oak tree.

Chapter 2
The White Witch

After she read the spell, she laid down clutching the piece of paper over her heart. There she dosed in and out of a light sleep as she was too anxious to truly fall deep asleep. As the night slowly passed all she could think about was how she was going to go to the magic shop first thing in the morning to obtain the ingredients so she could cast the spell as soon as she could. So much did she just want to go there right now and wait outside the door to be right there at the moment they opened. The anticipation was truly unbearable. She waited so long and now here it was moments away from it all happening. It all just was so overwhelming that she was in and out of bed pacing around her room all night long where right before daybreak she fell back into a light sleep. Then suddenly the sun broke through her window which woke her. She immediately jumped to her feet and rushed out of her bedroom door not even for a moment looking to see what time it was. All she knew is that it was finally daylight and she had to make it to the magic store. Out the front door she ran barely closing it behind her as she made her way down her street. As she got a few houses down she started to feel a strange feeling like someone was watching her. She looked around but everyone was still sleeping. Then suddenly she noticed a beautiful white cat with deep blue eyes sitting on the step of the little white house that sat on Pump Station Road right before Rainbow Road. It was such an uneasy feeling as it felt like the cat was just staring her down of which she just blew it off as she passed by the house. What was even stranger about it all was that she did not even realize that someone had moved into that house. For so long it was just vacant and not even up for sale. But nonetheless it did not matter as she continued down the street to where she was going. As she got to and made a left onto Rainbow Rd. she stopped for a moment to look at her love's house which sat on the corner of Rainbow Rd and Pumping Station Rd. It was such a wonderful house surrounded by a white picket fence. She whispered "I love you Ethan" as she made her way pass his house and down the street. Her pace quickened as she could see the cars traveling up and down Lynn Street ahead. As she approached the street she took a left and caught a glimpse of the Funeral home on her left which always touched her deepest emotions. The energy there was very profound and powerful of which she felt connected to. This pulled her energy for just a moment as she continued down Lynn Street toward the magic shop. She could feel her excitement grow as she was almost there as she could see the parking lot entrance just ahead. Once again her pace quickened but as she reached the shop she saw it was closed. How could this be she thought as for the first time she looked at the time and saw that it was only 6am and the shop did not open until 7:30am. This caused her to feel such a disappointment as she walked up to the darkened shop. She really could have sworn it was later. She stood there for a moment just staring into the shop windows. This was just so terrible that she had still wait to get what she wanted. With nothing better to do than just stand there waiting she decided to stop into the 7/11 that was right next store. At least she could get something to eat and drink while she waited she thought as she opened the store door. As she entered the store she went straight to the refrigerator door and grabbed a cold Pepsi. She then made her way to the candy and chip aisle and grabbed a four pack of Reeses cups, a bag of chips and a bag of pretzels and then headed to the cashier.

"Good morning, will this be all?" the cashier asked as she started ringing up the items.

"Yes," Gabriella replied.

"That would be $6 please" she said as she placed the items into a bag and handed it to Gabriella.

Gabriella reached into her pocket and pulled out a wrinkled up ten-dollar bill and handed it to the cashier.

"Thank you," the cashier said as she straightened the bill, stuck it into the cash register and took out the change and handed it to Gabriella. Gabriella did not say a thing as she headed out of the store and back to the magic shop. As she got back to the magic shop she looked back in through the window but still closed. She could see the clock on the wall and saw that she had another half hour before the shop opened. Frustrated she went to the bench that sat to the side of the shop window and sat down. She took out the chip and pretzels and opened both bags and placed them along the backrest of the bench so she could easily reach into each. She then took out the Reeses cups opening them and laying them on the bench next to her. She then took the soda out and placed it on the ground next to the bench. Slowly she started eating the chips and pretzels as she started to fade into her thoughts about how wonderful life was going to be with Ethan. All she could think about was how he was going to love her forever as she loves him. There she sat eating and drinking until suddenly she heard the door open where she leaped up and rushed to the door leaving all of her trash right there on the bench.

"Good morning Gabriella, how are you doing today?" the store keeper Mr. Qiquiang Nguyen asked as he took a step back to let her through the door.

"I am well" she barely replied as she made her way to the counter where she waited for Mr. Nguyen to arrive. As he got there he asked "what can I help you with today?"

"I need these items," as she handed him the piece of paper. Mr. Nguyen looked at the items and then at her as she anxiously waited.

"Is this really what you want Gabriella?" he asked with concern.

"Yes" she replied. "Why do you ask?"

"I have not seen these ingredients for a very long time" he calmly said.

"So what does that matter?" she forcefully said. "Will you ring me up or not?"

"Yes I will but these are ingredients of a very powerful spell which you should be very careful casting" he caringly replied.

"I really do not need your advice right now. I just need for you to give me what I came for."

"Yes Gabriella," Mr. Nguyen replied as he turned to gathered what she needed and then rang her up, placed the items in a bag and said "that will be $25 please".

She reached into her pocket pulled out the $25 and handed it to him and then grabbed the bag and rushed to the front door without so much as a thank you or goodbye.

Mr. Nguyen yelled to her as she was halfway out the door, "do you want your receipt?"

"No" she mumbled as the door closed behind her.

As she got outside with the bag tightly clinched in her hand she quickly started down the street toward the exotic pet store where she knew they had a love dove. The walk was about three miles from the magic shop but this did not deter her one little bit. She knew what she wanted and she was going to get it no matter what she had to do. So, on she went down Lynn Street to County Street and then zig zagged her way from street to street until she got to Sylvan Street where she finally arrived at the pet store. Without hesitation she walked through the big parking lot, straight through the store doors and right up to the bird cages. There in the very first cage were two beautiful love doves sitting peacefully next to each other in their cage. Gabriella looked around to find someone who could help her but could not find anyone close by. This frustrated her as she grew very impatient at no one being able to help her. After a very short moment she walked to the casher at the front of the store and walked right in front of everyone standing in line and said in a very demanding voice "I need someone to come help me with the birds."

The cashier startled by her aggression politely responded "someone will be right there" as she pick up the microphone and said "could we please have someone help a customer at the bird cages, thank you". She then turned back to Gabriella to ask if she needed anything else but Gabriella had already walked away back to the bird cages. There Gabriella once again stood in front of the cage staring at the love doves.

"Hello Miss, my name is Cindy. I am the store manager. Can I help you with something?" Gabriella heard the store manager ask.

"Yes I want to buy a male love dove" Gabriella responded without even looking in the managers' direction.

"I am very sorry, we do not sell just one of the love doves. They are a couple who mate for life and can only be sold together" the store manager responded.

"But I only need the male" Gabriella responded in frustration as she continued to stare at the birds.

"I am very sorry but if we split the couple they would both suffer from the sadness of missing the other. This is why we cannot sell them separately. They must be sold as a couple and remain together after the purchase." The store manager calmly explained.

"Fine then, how much do you want for the two of them and which one is the male?" Gabriella frustratingly said as she finally looked at the store manager.

"These two are on sale for $50 for the couple and the male is the light brown one," the store manager hesitatingly responded. Her gut was telling her not to sell these beautiful birds to Gabriella. She just had such a bad feeling about doing so but as the store manager she had no choice.

"Fine I will take them," Gabriella exclaimed.

"I will move them to a transportation cage for you and bring them to the cashier. Please meet me up there," the store manager said as she left to get the cage.

Without a word Gabriella headed to the cashier. After a few minutes of Gabriella impatiently waiting the store manager returned with the birds. The manager placed them on the counter next to the cashier and looked at Gabriella and caringly reminded her that the two birds must remain together.

"Yeah, I got it," Gabriella superficially responded and then paid for the birds grabbed the cage and left the store. The manager then turned to the cashier with tears in her eyes and said that she had such a bad feeling selling her those beautiful birds. The cashier also had tears in her eyes from the sale. Outside the store Gabriella quickly made her way back across the parking lot and back down the zig zagging streets that brought her to the pet store. She was so pumped up about it all that is felt like just a few minutes and there she was back on Ethan's street. As she made her way down the street she could feel her heart pound in her chest as she could see Ethan outside his house with his friends. The closer she got the more it felt like it was going to pound right out of her chest. She really loved him and just could not understand why he did not have feelings for her. So often has she made herself available to him but he just never showed any interest in her. But this was all about to change she thought to herself as she quietly passed by his house keeping him in view in the corner of her eye as he did not even notice her. As she got to the corner and turned onto her street there at the house with the white cat was a beautiful white-haired woman with long white hair and deep blue eyes. She could feel the woman staring at her but did not make eye contact with her. She also felt very uneasy with the woman as she did with the cat. She just sort of glanced out of the side of her eye in her direction as she continued down her street to her house. All she really cared about was getting to the house so she could get ready to cast the spell. As she rushed through the door she barely close the door behind her as she went straight to her bedroom and placed the birds and the bag on the floor in the corner of the room.

She then laid in her bed as the plan was to wait until the full moon of that night to cast the spell. This seemed to take forever as she impatiently waited in her room. As the night fell and she could see the light from the full moon pouring through her window she grabbed the cage and the bag and headed to the kitchen. There she removed the jar from the bag and filled it with water. She then grabbed the butcher knife from the drawer and quickly gathered everything and headed outside to the clearing behind the pool in her back yard. It was like the light of day in the clearing as the harvest full moon lit up everything. As she got to the center of the clearing she placed everything on the ground and sat down beside it. She then grabbed the jar, placed it in front of her, took the lid off and then added in the 6 rose petals, 6 rosemary leaves, 6 catnip leaves, her treasured cats eye gemstone, and a picture of Ethan that she cut out of the school year book. She then looked over to the cage. The birds were nervously together in the back of the cage. She then reached in and tried to grab the male. The birds started chirping and jumping away from her hand. She finally trapped the male against the side of the cage and yanked him out of the cage leaving the cage door open. The male bird tried to peck at her hand but could not reach it. The female left the cage and was now off to the side of Gabriella chirping but Gabriella paid no mind to her as she reached for the knife and slit the throat of the bird and let the blood drip into the jar. The female bird instantly started to chirp in sadness as you could feel her despair overwhelm her. Gabriella paid no mind to the female as she tossed the dead male love dove into the woods behind her, closed the jar, gathered everything up and went into the house. The female love dove flew over to where Gabriella threw the male and sat on the tree branch next to the body. There she sat quietly chirping to the male love dove. As Gabriella entered the house she threw the butcher knife into the kitchen sink and immediately went into her room. Once in the room she went straight to the altar and placed the jar in between the three candles. She then sat on the side of her bed staring at the altar without making a move for hours. As the day broke she got up and went into the kitchen to get something to eat. Her mother was already there at the kitchen table having a cup of coffee.

"Good morning Gabriella," her mother said as she took a sip of her coffee.

"Morning," Gabriella halfheartedly responded.

"Did you cut yourself on that knife you left in the sink?"

"No, I cut me a piece of steak last night,"

"It was disgusting that you just left a bloody knife in the sink without washing it. It took forever to get it clean."

"It is cleaned now right so stop complaining," Gabriella sarcastically said as she grabbed a soda and walked back to her room. The four days passed slow as Gabriella spent most of the time in her room staring at the altar. Through the open window she could hear the female love dove still chirping which she really did not pay any mind to. Finally the 5th day arrived and at midnight she lit the three candles and started to chant three times;

> By the power below and above,
> I am asking you to bring me love.
> By this spell that I have cast,
> I want a love that will always last.

> By the power below and above,
> I am asking you to bring me love.
> By this spell that I have cast,
> I want a love that will always last.

> By the power below and above,
> I am asking you to bring me love.
> By this spell that I have cast,
> I want a love that will always last.

Gabriella stayed in her room the whole 5th day making sure the candles did not go out. As midnight of the 6th day arrived, she could feel the energy of the spell fill the room. This filled her with excitement as she just knew in the morning she would be loved by Ethan. As the morning broke, she went out, crossed the street and headed straight to Ethan's house. As she got close to the corner where Ethan's house was there was that white haired woman sitting on her porch starring at her again. This started to bother Gabriella very much as she gave the woman a cold hard stare back as she continued to walk to house Ethan's. As Gabriella reached the corner of where Ethan's house was there was Ethan sitting on the step of his house. As soon as he saw Gabriella he leaped up and headed straight for her.

"Good morning Gabriella. How are you feeling this morning?" he dotingly asked.

"I am well," Gabriella answered.

"Are you heading somewhere?"

"Yes, I am going to the store."

"Do you mind if I tag along with you?"

"No," Gabriella replied as they both continued down the street together. Gabriella was beside herself with joy that here she was finally with the love of her life as they walked together to the store. The whole way all Ethan could talk about was how he woke this morning with nothing but feelings and thoughts for her. He could not understand how he never noticed how in love he was with her as he reached out to hold her hand as he told her how beautiful her dark brown hair and eyes were. Gabriella was just so happy that she did not say a word as all he did was go on and on about how beautiful and wonderful she is. As they arrived at and entered the store Ethan asked what she wanted and she said "Just a soda."

"What kind?"

"Pepsi please."

Together they walked to the refrigerator where Ethan reached in and pulled out two Pepsi's and then they walked to the cashier. They then left the store and heading back toward Ethan's house. As they got to Ethan's house he asked "would you like to stop in?"

"Very much," Gabriella happily replied as they headed to his house. As they entered the house Ethan's mother greeted them as she gave Ethan a hug and asked how he was doing.

"I am very well mom," Ethan replied.

"And who do you have with you," his mom asked as she reached out to Gabriella to shake her hand.

"This is Gabriella."

"It is very nice to meet you Gabriella," mom said with a big smile.

"Thank you," Gabriella hesitantly replied as she really was not use to such family interaction. Her mom and dad barely spoke to her let alone gave hugs and smiles.

"We are going to hangout a little," Ethan happily said as he took Gabriella by the hand to his room.

"Okay, just let me know if you need anything," his mom shouted as they left the room.

Gabriella was a little overwhelmed by all of this but really did not care all that much for she had all she ever wanted with Ethan giving her so much attention. The rest of the day they just hung out in Ethan's room where all he talked about was how much he loved her and wanted her. After a while there was a knock on Ethan's door.

"Yes, who is it," Ethan asked.

"It's mom. It is time for dinner. Will Gabriella be eating with us?"

Ethan looked at Gabriella and asked, "Please stay for dinner."

Gabriella did not know how to respond at first for she really was not ready for all the family stuff but then said, "No I have to be going."

"Oh please stay," Ethan begged.

"I am sorry but I have to go."

"Don't pressure her Ethan," mom said from the other side of the door.

"Okay but when will I see you again?" Ethan asked Gabriella.

"In the morning we can take another walk if you want."

"Oh yes but that is so long from now. I will miss you so much," Ethan said as he gently kissed her on the lips and whispered "please say you will be mine forever."

"I will love you forever," she so happily replied as she headed to the bedroom door with Ethan holding her hand the whole way. As they left the room his mom asked again "are you sure you do not want to stay for dinner Gabriella?"

"No I have to get home now," she emotionlessly said as she and Ethan continued to the front door.

"Good bye Gabriella. Take care," mom said as Ethan opened the door.

"Good bye," Gabriella replied as she walked out the door with Ethan in tow.

As they got outside she turned to say goodbye but as soon as she did Ethan kissed her right on the lips. For a long moment there they stayed locked in the most passionate kiss she have ever felt. As the kiss ended Ethan looked her right in the eyes and whispered "I love you so much."

Gabriella breathless whispered back "I love you so very much," as she turned and headed home. As she left Ethan's and crossed the street and made the turn onto her street there was the white-haired woman still sitting on her porch staring at Gabriella. Without even thinking about it Gabriella gave her the finger. The woman did not say a word as she just kept staring at Gabriella walking by. As Gabriella got to her house she caught out the side of her eye that the woman was no longer there and instead the white cat was now sitting on the porch. Gabriella just really did not care about any of this for all she could really feel was how happy she was now that she had Ethan's love as she opened the door and walked in straight to her bedroom where she fell asleep dreaming of Ethan and her.

Chapter 3

The Gypsies

The next day Gabriella woke bright and early, jumped into the shower, threw on some clothes and headed right out the door to go see Ethan. As she opened the door there was Ethan standing on the door step waiting for her.

"Good morning my precious love," Ethan said with a smile on his face as he took her by the hand and gave her a soft tender kiss on her lips.

"Good morning," Gabriella whispered from within her smile.

"How are you feeling this wonderful morning?"

"I am well and you?"

"As happy as I can be from within the love of you. I thought it would be a beautiful day for us to take a walk to the lake," he joyfully expressed.

"That would be so wonderful," she said as she walked out to him while closing the door behind her.

Ethan did not for a moment let go of her hand as they turned and hand in hand walked down the street to the end of Pump Station Rd. Gabriella was so engulfed in the moment that she did not even see the white cat sitting on the porch staring at them as they passed the white haired woman's house. As they got to the end of the street they made a right onto the road leading to the cemetery and then another right at the flag pole with the American flag that led them into the cemetery. They then followed the road through the cemetery to the lake. At the lake they went onto the dirt road that ran alongside the lake. The same one that Gabriella took to find the witch. As they made their way down the road Ethan stopped and gave Gabriella a deep passionate kiss. Gabriella could feel her soul melt into her heart as she could feel Ethan's want for her. The kiss felt like forever to Gabrielle as they stood locked in the passion of it. As their lips parted Ethan gazed into her eyes and whispered "I am so in love with you. I will never ever not be in love with you. You are my forever, my true love, my twin soul that I have waited so long to have. You are my everything". She was just so elated that she did not want this moment to ever end. There they stood in an embrace that felt more wonderful than she could ever imagine in a moment that truly had no sense of time. They truly could not be happier. After what felt like an eternity of happiness within their embrace they turned and continued down the road. As they passed the boulder which led to the witch Gabriella glanced in that direction as she squeezed Ethan's hand a little bit tighter. As they continued down the path Ethan turned to her and said "you are the most beautiful part of my life. You bring so much joy to everything that is of me. My heart smiles only because of you. I cherish the very essence of which is you in my life."

Gabriella just walked beside him holding his hand tight as she just let the words fill her heart.

A little further down the path they turned onto the walkway that led across the lake. As they got halfway across they sat down on the side of the path. As they sat there gazing across the lake. Ethan asked Gabriella if she wanted to hear a poem that he had written for her.

"Oh yes very much," she replied.

"I hope you like it," Ethan modestly said as he expressed his poem to her.

Eternally Forever

To you I give
For as long as I may live
My mind, body, heart and soul
Unconditionally and without control

This I freely do
With all that I am just for you
For what I am so very sure of
Is that what is between us is a forever true love

Such is what I want to be
You and me in this love for eternity

Sharing that of what true love is all about

From within the feeling that with each other we just cannot be without

"So beautiful," Gabriella joyful said as Ethan finished.

"I cannot stop thinking about you and how much I love you. You are all I can feel. You flow through me as if you were my blood," Ethan said with all the love he had for her.

There they sat hand in hand throughout the rest of the day and into the night as the full moon lit up the entire area. The moment was just so wonderfully romantic that they did not even realize that they sat there the entire night and into the next morning. As the sun rouse over the lake Ethan reached over and kissed Gabriella and again told her how much he loves her and asked "are you hungry?"

"Yes, a little," she replied.

"Do you want to come to my house for some breakfast?"

"That would be nice."

"Okay then let's go to my house."

"Okay," she said as they both stood up and headed hand in hand down the walkway to the other side of the lake from which they came. As they got to the end of the walkway, they made their way down the small hill to the grass path between the lake and the tree line. There they made the way along the side of the lake. As they got about half-way down the path Ethan stopped and pulled her close to him. She again could feel his want for her as they started to kiss. Together they began to moan as they fell to the grass. Together they started to rip the clothes from each other and as if there was no one else in the world but them they made passionate love to each other. Without any sense of time, they laid there exhausted and satisfied within each other's embrace. After some time, Ethan whispered "are you ready to go?"

"Give me a few more moments within your love," she replied.

"Okay my love," he answered.

As the time passed, they just held each other without a word. After quite some time they rouse from the grass and slowly got dressed. They then started back down the path and through the streets to Ethan's house. As they got closer to his house they could see his mother standing on the step visibly upset. As they approached the house she asked in a nervous voice "what is wrong with you? Where were you all night? I was worried sick about you."

"I am so sorry mom. We just lost track of time."

"Please just get in the house," she said with anger and concern in her voice.

"Gabriella and I are hungry and I invited her for breakfast," he said as he held Gabriella's hand tight.

"Not today, just get in the house and let Gabriella go home."

"No, I want to have breakfast with her."

"What has gotten into you? This is not like you. Please just get in the house."

"I will not..." just as Gabriella interrupted.

"Maybe it is best I go home Ethan. We can catch up later. I really need to take a shower anyway."

"Are you sure?"

"Yes I am. You go in for now and we will catch up later."

"Okay my love but I will miss you," he said as he reached over and kissed her.

They then let go of each other's hand and Gabriella started to walk home as Ethan went into the house. Gabriella turned and took one last look and saw Ethan's mom walking in behind him and closing the door behind them. Gabriella then turned back around and there on the step was that white haired woman again staring at her. "I have had enough of you," yelled Gabriella. "What in the fuck are you staring at bitch? I am really sick and tired of your constant staring at me every time I pass your godforsaken home," she said with all the anger she had inside of her. "If you continue eyeballing me I am going to kick your fucking ass," she yelled as she continued pass the woman's house and down the street to her house. She then turned to yell at her some more but when she did the woman was gone and the white cat was sitting there. "Fuck you both. Really fuck you both," was all she could say as she went into her house, to the shower and then to bed. She fell asleep quick but could not stay asleep. After a few hours she woke full of thoughts about Ethan and very hungry. She went to the kitchen and made herself a sandwich and grabbed a bag of chips, a Pepsi and headed to the computer. She sat down, turned the computer on and started to eat. As soon as the computer was on a message from Skype came up from Ethan asking to connect. Quickly she accepted and there was Ethan asking to do a video chat. She quickly clicked to connect and there he was smiling at her. "Hi my wonderful love. I missed you so much," he said with all of his heart.

"I missed you also," she responded with a smile.

"I cannot wait to be with you gain. I so long to touch you, to kiss you, to hold you in my arms again and be with you every moment of every moment always and forever," he said with such a passionate energy. "Please check your email. I sent you some poetry that I wrote for you. You and this love I feel for you is just so inspirational that I cannot stop thinking about you and feeling you which just pours out of me in so many poetic ways," he excitedly said.

"Okay," she said as she opened her email and saw 30 poems from him. She then started reading the first one to herself.

"Please read it to me so I can hear your beautiful voice express my feelings for you," he asked.

"Okay," she said as she started reading the first one from the beginning.

Pleasingly Pleasing You

I want to hold you all through the night
And kiss you at the morning's light
Then spend the whole day
Pleasing you in every way

I want this only with you
My whole life through
Anyhow anywhere anytime
Every moment until the end of time

This is the life I want to live
Where to you, all of me and everything I give
From within a love so true and pure
Where the delight of your heart, soul, mind and body I so gently explore

"Thank you so much," she said as she finished reading it.

"You are so welcomed. You are truly my forever love," he said with all of his heart.

They chatted for a few hours more as Ethan continually expressed his undying love for her. Around midnight he asked if he could come over to be with her.

"Please do but what about your mother. Isn't she mad at you?" she asked.

"She will be asleep by then and will not even know. I will be over in a few moments."

"Okay. Come to my bedroom window," she joyfully answered.

In less than a moment there was Ethan at her bedroom window which Gabriella had opened for him. "Hi love," he said as he crawled through the window. "I missed you so much," he said as he took her in his arms.

"I missed you so much," she said as they fell to the bed and passionately made love to each other for the rest of the night. The next day they got up and went to the kitchen to grab something to eat. The house was really quiet for everyone had already left for the day.

"Wow, your house is really quiet," Ethan said.

"Yes, it is always like this. Rarely is anyone home," she responded as she grabbed the bowls, spoons, cereal and milk. There they sat eating and talking with most of the conversation being Ethan expressing his love for her. After about an hour or so Ethan sadly expressed that he better get back home. Gabriella agreed.

"I will miss you so much," Ethan expressed.

"I will miss you also," Gabriella sadly responded as he headed to her front door with her right beside him and him holding her hand.

As they got to the door they kissed and hug as he said "I really do not want to go."

"I really do not want you to go," she responded.

There they stood kissing and hugging for quite a while as neither wanted to let go of the other.

"I guess I should get back home," he sadly said as they continued to kiss and hug.

"I know," she sadly said as they just kept kissing and hugging.

"I really should be on my way."

"Yes you should."

This went on for some time as he slowly made it out the door. As he got on the steps he turned and said once again "I am going to miss you so much."

"As I you," she responded as he slowly made his way down the steps.

Ethan slowly made his way down the street to his house. Gabriella stood on the steps and watched him until he was out of sight. She then turned to go into her house but out the side of her eye she saw the white-haired woman staring at her from the steps of her house. Gabriella stopped for a moment, flipped her off and then went into the house.

By this time Ethan had made it to his window and was quietly sneaking through it. Just as he got through the window his mother was right there at the door.

"Where have you been? I was ready to call the police on you. This is not like you. What has gotten into you Ethan?" she asked with tears in her eyes and concern in her voice.

"I was okay. I just went out. You worry too much," he responded without any care whatsoever about her feelings.

"It is that girl that is doing this to you. She is trouble and a bad influence on you," she angrily expressed.

"I love her and there is nothing wrong with her," he defiantly responded.

"Ever since you have been with her you have changed. This is truly not good. I forbid you to see her anymore. Your father and I will talk to you about this tonight," she sadly expressed.

"I do not care what anyone says, I will be with her. I love her with all of my heart and soul and no one can keep us apart. She is my true forever love," he yelled back at her.

The rest of the day Ethan remained in his room Skyping with Gabriella. All he could do is want her. The desire was overwhelming. He could not think of or feel anything else but her. They spent the whole time with him reading his poetry to her and him telling her how he could never be without her ever. Suddenly there was a knock at the bedroom door. Ethan did not acknowledge it at all as he just kept talking to Gabriella. There was a knock again and then the door opened and his father walked in. "Hey guy, your mother and I would like to speak to you."

"I am busy right now," Ethan said without even looking in his father's direction.

"Please turn off your laptop and come with me. It is important that we speak with you," his father calmly expressed.

"Fine, I hope this will not take long. I am right in the middle of something," Ethan responded as he pushed his laptop to the side, got up and stormed through the door.

His father followed him but just as he got to the door turned and looked at the laptop and there was Gabriella on the screen quietly watching it all. He then turned and walked out closing the door behind him. As he got to the kitchen there was Ethan's mother leaning against the counter with tears in her eyes and Ethan sitting at the table visibly angry.

"Son, is everything okay?" he asked.

"I am really tired of everyone asking me that. I am fine," Ethan said in frustration.

"It really does not seem like you are okay Ethan. You do not seem like yourself. Something really seems wrong. Your mother thinks it has something to do with a girl you have been seeing," his father caring said.

"She is wrong. There is nothing wrong with me and there is nothing wrong with me seeing Gabriella. I love her very much and that will never change. She is my true love and I will do anything for her and there is nothing wrong with that. I am in love with her," Ethan defiantly said.

"We understand being in love Ethan but love is supposed to bring out the best of someone and this love for this girl does not seem to bring out the best in you. It seems to have changed you in a way that makes you nervous and on edge," his father tried to explain.

"You really do not know what you are talking about. You really do not know what it means to be in love as I am. You really need to mind your own business and stay out of my life," he yelled as he stormed out of the house.

All Ethan's mother could do is break down in tears as his father took her in his arms to somehow comfort her. They both were completely confused of why Ethan was acting this way. He was always the perfect son. Over the next few months Ethan got worse and worse with staying away from the home, staying in his room when he was home and arguing with his parents all the time. All he could feel was his feelings for Gabriella. All he could want to do was be with Gabriella whether it was on Skype, WhatsApp, texting, phone, Facebook or physically. This all went on for a couple years where as the months turned into years Ethan's whole life was affected. His grades at school drop. He gave up sports and all of his hobbies. He abandoned his friends and became more and more distant from his family. Ethan was either with Gabriella in one way or another or writing love poems about his love for her. He truly had no interest in anything else unless it had something to do with Gabriella and Gabriella had no problem with this. In fact as the years passed she kept him closer and closer to her side. She controlled Ethan's entire life and everything they did and everywhere they went. This was mainly because she was so worried about what the witch said about the spell being broken by a true love. She did not let him out of her sight for a moment. If she even caught sight of another girl she rushed him into another direction. Ethan's family and friends tried their best to convince him that this was not good for him but he would not listen to a word of it and would get very aggressive and defensive if they pushed it too hard. Eventually his friends just sort of gave up and faded away and his family just kept trying to be there for him within their sadness of what this all had done to him and to their family. One day, as usual, Ethan was rushing out the front door with his mother trying to get him to stop to eat. "Please Ethan eat something before you run out."

"I do not have time," he yelled as he slammed the front door behind him as his mother gave a heavy sigh for she had no more tears to cry. As Ethan got outside he rushed straight to Gabriella's house as fast as he could for today was a big day—it was Gabriella's 18th birthday. When he arrived at her door he opened it and walked right in. As usual the house was very quiet for no one was home but Gabriella. He first went to the refrigerator and grabbed a Pepsi for Gabriella for she liked a cold Pepsi to start her day. He then went to her bedroom where she was lying on the bed. "Good morning beautiful. Happy birthday," he said as he handed her the Pepsi and the gift he made for her as he crawled into bed next to her. "I missed you so much," he said as he took her in his arms.

"Good morning handsome. So wonderful that you remembered my birthday," she said.

Ethan so excited by it all gently started to kiss her as she tried to un-wrap the gift.

"That tickles," she giggled as he kissed her everywhere he could reach.

"I just love you so very much my forever love," he said between the kisses.

She was so distracted by the kisses that she had such a hard time opening the gift. "Wait, I want to see the gift," she hesitantly said.

"Okay," he said as he kissed her even more until she finally got the gift opened.

"Oh my God a manuscript of your poetry," she said with tears in her eyes as she flipped through the pages.

"Yes my love. All inspired by you and my love for you," he lovingly said.

"Please read me one," she said as she handed it to him.

"Okay," he said as he took it and flipped to one of the pages.

Why Otherwise

I could do so many things
Of what life brings
Each and every day
In every little way

The possibilities have no end
From hanging with a crowd to making a wonderful new friend
Or to just ease back and learn another song to sing
To being somewhere to someone some kind of king

But as wonderful as it would all be to do
All I really want to do is to be with you
For why would I want to do anything otherwise
When my life is fulfilled whenever I gaze into your eyes

"That was so beautiful," she whispered.

"I love you so much. I cannot be without you ever. You are my forever true love," he whispered as their bodies pulled to each other in want. There they spent the rest of the morning making love. Around noon Gabriella turned to Ethan and said "Let's go to the magic shop. I have to get some items that I am getting ready to run out of." Gabriella actually spent a lot of time at the magic shop. Since casting the first spell she become more and more depended on casting spells for anything she wanted or did not want.

"Are you sure? How about we just stay right here for the rest of the day making love?" he asked as he took her in his arms and started kissing her.

"I would want nothing more than to do so but I really need the items," she reluctantly replied. "If we get it out of the way now, we will have the rest of the day to ourselves."

"Okay but let's do it fast so I can make some more beautiful love with you for the rest of the day."

"Okay my love," as they got out of bed, got dressed and headed out the door. As they walked down the street hand in hand Gabriella noticed out the side of her eye the white-haired woman standing in her door way. God, I hate that woman she said as she they passed her house. "That is Ariana. She is a nice lady," Ethan said.

"You know her?"

"Yes, I met her when she moved in. She is truly a very nice lady."

"I don't want you to be around her. I do not like her," Gabriella quickly said as she turned to him.

"Okay," he responded without hesitation as they continued down the street. This made her very happy that he listened to her as she thought to herself how this was such a perfect day with everything going her way which caused her to squeeze his hand a little tighter. He in turn squeezed back as they happily walked down the streets to the magic shop like there was no one else in the world. But as they passed the people on the street Gabriella started feeling the cold stares of the others around them. This started to make her feel uneasy as she started staring back at them. Quickly would they look away from her cold hearted stare at them. They did not know what is was about her and what hold she had on Ethan but they were too afraid of her to push it too far. All they could manage to do was talk behind her back about how they did not belong together. Gabriella really did not care too much about them and their feelings and thoughts about her as long as they kept their distance from Ethan. She knew the risk and made sure to control everything and everyone. As they got closer to the magic shop Gabriella started focusing on the items that she needed. It has been a while since she has been to the shop and was running out of items that helped to cast some of her more powerful spells. She started feeling more in control and once again happy again as they reached the shop when all of a sudden her body started trembling for no reason at all. She could feel that something was serious wrong with the energies. She quickly looked around where she caught sight of two gypsies, a weathered beaten man dressed in black with a black leather bandana and a young girl by his side staring at her. She could feel the natural power of the two dominate over hers. She got drawn into staring back at them as she somehow felt disconnected from everything real and did not even realize that she let go of Ethan's hand. At this very moment Ethan saw a beautiful crystal in a display outside of the shop and thought that this would be such a beautiful gift for Gabriella. His excitement overwhelmed him as he rushed over to get it for Gabriella. As he reached for the crystal so did a woman at the very same time. Just as this was happening the man and young girl broke their stare with Gabriella where Gabriella broke free of the trance she was in just in time to see Ethan and the woman about to touch. Gabriella screamed but it was too late. They touched and they instantaneously connected as they gazed into each other eyes. Immediately there was a shift of energies as Ethan and the woman became engulfed within each other. Gabriella overwhelmed by the shift screamed in emotional pain as she could feel that the spell was broken. She was devastated. Her whole world came to an end. She quickly looked back at the man and the girl to blame but they were gone like they were never there. She turned back to Ethan and the woman and saw them just gazing into each other. She could hear their conversation as Ethan said "Hi my name is Ethan. It is very nice to meet you and the woman said "Hi my name is Jenna. It is very nice to meet you," as they both continued to gaze at each other. All Gabriella could do is let out a scream that shook the buildings. Ethan and the woman both looked in the direction of the scream and there sitting in the middle of the parking lot was a pitch black cat meowing the saddest meow you could hear.

"Oh, such a poor kitty. She must be lost. I hope she does not get hit by a car," Jenna caringly said.

"She for sure looks like she can take care of herself. She has such a mean look," Ethan said as he took a quick look at the cat and then back at Jenna. "Would you like to go get an ICEE?" he asked.

"I would love to," she responded as they slowly walked off together as the black cat painfully meowed that much louder.

Chapter 4

The Black Witch

There the black cat sat painfully meowing when suddenly a car came racing into the parking lot blowing its horn. The cat hissed at the car as it swerved around her. As the man looked in the rearview mirror to see if he hit the cat all he saw was Gabriella standing there. As she turned her head to look at the car all four tires blew out. The man did everything he could not to lose control of the car. Gabriella turned and headed to the magic shop. As she entered Mr. Nguyen looked up from stocking the shelf and immediately saw Gabriella had changed. Her hair was now pitch black and her eyes were such a dark brown that they almost looked black. He knew that the spell was broken and she was in a deep heartache as neither of them said a word. Gabriella just went about gathered the things she needed and headed to the checkout where Mr. Nguyen was already there waiting on her.

"Is everything alright Gabriella?" he hesitantly asked.

She just stared at him with a dead look in her eyes.

"The spell was broken, wasn't it?" he asked.

She did not reply. She just stood there staring straight through him as he rang up the purchase.

"I know it hurts Gabriella but you need to try to get a hold on yourself. You cannot allow this to take control over you," he said with concern for he knew what she was capable of doing from within such heartache.

Still she said nothing as he finished ringing up and packing her order. She then paid, grabbed her stuff and left without as much as a word spoken. As she walked down the streets that she and Ethan had walked together so often the hurt turned more and more into a deep burning anger. All she could think about and feel was how fucked up it was that that man and girl was right there at that very moment. For sure she would kill them if she ever saw them again. After a moment or so her thoughts and feelings turned to that girl that just happened to be there at that very moment that Ethan was out of her control. Such a bitch, she could have been anywhere else in the world except right there right then she thought. Her hate for her was immediate and strong. She did not deserve Ethan. No one deserved him for he belonged to her in an eternal love she told herself. As thoughts and feelings continued her anger grew more and more at everyone. There was Ethan's mother and father who never accepted her and their love. There were Ethan's friends who never allowed her to be a part of them. All she could think about was how she wanted to make everyone suffer for this happening as she made her way to her house. As she reached the door of her house the door flew open all by itself with a mighty force. She walked into the house as the door slammed shut behind her. As she made her way to her bedroom all the furniture within the house was forced out of her way. Her negative angry energy by this time had become a strong vibration that was pulsating from her like a wave disrupting everything in her path. As she entered her room the door slammed behind her and her spell book flew into her hand. There she stayed in her room for days as her anger grew into a hateful rage that she did not even attempt to control. After a week or so she finally went out of the house. As she walked down the street and passed by Ethan's house she could see Ethan and Jenna sitting outside holding hands and kissing. This infuriated her more and more causing her rage to burn deep inside of her. As the next few weeks passed it all got worse and worse where Ethan and Jenna became the perfect couple with Ethan becoming the well-adjusted person that he once was. This made his family so happy to have him back to his old self where they embrace Jenna as part of the family. Even Ethan's friends started coming back around again where Jenna fit right into the group. Ethan even started playing sports again and getting back into all of his hobbies. You could visibly see the happiness fill him and everyone. It was like a bright light was shining on the house making everyone and everything glow with joy. This made Gabriella's darkness that much more evident and profound. Every time she even caught a glimpse of it all it made her sink deeper into the darkness of hate and anger. Everything about her just became negative and black. What made it all that much more worse was that Ethan did not even notice her and what she was going through in the least little bit. It was like the relationship with her never even happened. She could feel deep within her how this weighed heavy on her soul so much that it brought emotional and physical pain to her. It was such a pain that she could not hide from or overcome it of which left her feeling engulfed by only the dreed of every breath she took and every moment she was in. All she could feel was how this all ripped the life out of her leaving only the hatred of everything and everybody and how she was going to make them pay for it. As the months passed Gabriella fell deep into the darkness of negative energy. This surrounded her so much that it became who she was in the eyes of everyone. What was once just her being someone that others saw as a troubled soul was now someone that everyone avoided and shunned as a force of evil. This only served to make her that much more angry, hateful and revengeful without the will to be anything else. One day as she was walking to the magic shop she caught sight of Ethan and Jenna playing around with each other. As they walked down the street hand in hand next to each other they would bump into each other and say "crash baby" and laugh as they would safely hold each other tight by the hand from falling. Watching this made Gabriella feel sick throughout her whole being so much that all she could do was wish them both harm. Later that evening, as she was falling deeper into the darkness of her negative hatred, she started conjuring the thoughts of how to inflict the revenge she needed to see them all feel. Quickly she started flipping through the pages of her spell book and there it was in the pages between the pages. As soon as she saw it she knew that this was the perfect spell to extract her vengeance. The next day she rushed out to get the ingredients she needed. First she went to the graveyard to get some graveyard dirt and then she went to the street where she knew Ethan and Jenna walked every day where she waited for them. As usual they walked down the street playing "crash baby." When they got close enough she snapped a pic of them playing "crash baby" on her IPhone. She then headed over to the magic shop to purchase rain water, rat tail and green ink. She then rushed back to her house and into her room laying everything out on her bed. She then printed out the pic and laid it on the bed. That night she went out to the clearing in her yard and started a fire under her cauldron. She then added the rain water and then let some drops of green ink fall into the rain water until the water turned a dark green and then threw in the graveyard dirt, the rat tail and then the ashes of the photo. She then chanted,

"I am to avenge myself.
An old drama has happened here,
let it be once more,
let the loss of love happen again and again!
I take my revenge upon you."

She could feel the revenge burn in her throughout the night as the green water boiled over the red hot fire. At the break of day she rouse from the side of the cauldron, left the yard and headed to the street where she knew Ethan and Jenna would play their game. With her hatred still fuming with the anger of revenge she stood where she could watch them come. After a while of her waiting she caught sight of them walking hand in hand down the street. Her anger grew as they once again started their stupid little game as she could hear their stupid little words as they bumped into each other, "Crash Baby." However this time without them feeling it the spell caused them to start bumping into each other harder and harder when all of a sudden it was so hard that they loss their grip of each other's hand. Ethan could feel a pain in his heart as he could hear Jenna scream as she started to fall into the street. As their eyes connected, he could see the fear in her eyes as he quickly reached for her. But with their fingers just out of reach of each other he could not catch her as she fell right in front of a speeding car. The whole moment was like it was moving in slow motion as the car hit her and threw her into the air. As she fell back to the street Ethan rushed to her side as she lied there battered. "Oh my God. Oh my God call 911," he screamed as he took her lifeless body into his arms. "Please Jenna don't leave me," he cried. "Please Jenna stay with me," as his tears fell from his eyes. "Please, please help us," he cried out. The pain was just so unbearable for him. All he could do was just sit there embracing her body as he rocked back and forth in emotional pain. With agony in his heart he buried his face into her body and cried "Please Jenna I need you so much. Please don't leave me," For what seemed like forever within a moment there he sat with his face buried into her body as off to the side Gabriella just stood there with vengeance in her eyes watching Ethan crying his heart out. But his agonizing suffering just once was not enough to satisfy her vengeance. His suffering had to be more than just this one moment. It had to be over and over for an eternity for her heartache was without end so nor should his be. And just as Gabriella was ready to conjure the second part of the spell Ariana called out to her from across the street, "Stop now Gabriella. You caused enough heartache."

Gabriella looked at her in hate and then back at Ethan and then uttered the words, "So mote it be!" and the rest of the spell was casted sending Ethan, Jenna and Gabriella to the year 1944 Nazi Germany.

Ethan oblivious to everything else around him sobbed uncontrollably but then as he looked up with his blood stained face he saw people were running in every direction. He sat there for a moment looking around at it all when Gabriella, which everyone saw as a German Officer, started yelling at him in German to "move move get them." With a rifle in hand he quickly jumped to his feet and started running down a side street after a small group. It was the dark of night and you could hear gun shots in the distant as he yelled in German "come out now," but to no avail. He again shouted "come out now," as he heard a noise off to the side of him. Slowly he made his way to where the noise came from. "Come out now," he yelled as he moved a trash can from his view to reveal a young woman cowering along the wall. "Get up," get up he yelled with his rifle pointing at her but all she could do was cower there shaking to the bone. "Get up now," he yelled again as he reached down and grabbed her by the arm as she looked up at him with tears in her eyes. Immediately as he touched her and their eyes connected he could feel his love for her. It was truly overwhelming to feel such a deep feeling of love. This captivated them for a moment as they gazed into each other's eyes until his commanders voice broke the moment as he said "Good job, you caught one of those filthy pigs." This startled them as the commander reached over and pulled her from his grip. Ethan was speechless as the commander drug her down the street and into the waiting truck filled with other prisoners. Ethan just stood there in silence as the truck pulled away. The commander then came to him and told him great job and that it was time to go back to the camp. Ethan said nothing as he walked to the jeep and got in as it headed off to the camp. As the jeep got to the camp Ethan could see the girl being escorted by gun point into the fenced in area where she was processed and sent to a barracks. The next day Ethan quickly made his way to the fenced in area. At first he could not see the woman anywhere but then out the corner of his eye he saw her walking back to her barracks with a bucket of water. He could feel his heart pounding as he watched her walk. He could not believe how beautiful she was to him. She was like an angel in flight as she made her way through the door. Ethan just stood there staring at the door as his thoughts and feelings ran wild for this woman. Later the day Ethan made his way back to the fence line where he could see the woman walking around outside with the others. He then walked through the gate of the fence and straight to her and asked, "Are you okay?"

"Yes I am," she responded.

"Good I was worried about you," he said as they gazed into each other's eyes. It was like no one else existed as they just stood there talking. After a few moments Ethan said that he had to go.

"Will I see you again?" she asked.

"Yes," he responded as they continued gazing into each other. After a few minutes of this Ethan turned and headed out.

As he left she called after him "What is your name?"

"Ethan. What is yours?" he asked as he turned slightly toward her.

"Jenna."

"Such a beautiful name for such a beautiful woman," he responded as he made his way through the gate. Over the next few days which turned into weeks and then months Ethan did everything possible to be with her and to take care of her. Each moment with her was everything wonderful where they fell deeper and deeper into love. The time with her was everything he wanted in life. He could not stand to not be with her every moment of every moment. She was all he thought about, all he could feel. One day as he made his way to her she could see the worry on his face. As he got to her she asked, "Why do you worry?

"The enemy is approaching and I am worried what will happen. The commander said that he will not allow the camp to be taken. He said that he rather he and everyone at the camp would die first," Ethan said with a heavy heart.

"What will we do?" Jenna asked.

"We need to escape this place."

"How? When?"

"Tomorrow night. I will set it up and come get you." That night Ethan set it up where he would take the place of the back gate guard. He then left the camp and made the arrangements with the resistance where they would have safe passage to the nearby town and then hide out within their underground railroad. As he made his way back to the camp he thought about the plan where he would wait until midnight and then get her so they could make their way to the back gate and then out into the woods where they would run to a safe house. As he slowly walked through the woods in deep thought of it all he suddenly heard gunfire coming from the direction of the camp. He could feel his heart pound so hard that he thought it would jump right out of his chest as his pace started to quicken. "What was happening," he asked himself as his mind kept him from thinking the worse as his pace quickened into a full run. As he got close to the camp he stopped behind a tree to see what was going on. There across from him right outside of the camp he could see the American Army in battle with the guards. He did not know what to do as he was cut off when suddenly there was a large explosion the blast a hole in the fence right in front of him. Without hesitation he quickly ran straight for the hole as a crossfire of bullets flew all around him. This did not deter him a bit even as a bullet grazed his arm. All he could think about was how he had to make it to Jenna as he could hear the Americans shouting to halt as another bullet whistled right pass his head. As he got closer to the fence he could see his comrades laying down gunfire to protect him as he made his way through the hole and safely into the camp. He did not so much as slow down as he made his way to Jenna's barracks and straight through the door. Inside he called out, "Jenna, where are you?" But in return there was total silence. Again he cried out, "Jenna, where are you?" But once again silence. He could feel his heart ache as he did not know what to do to find her as he turned and headed to the door. Then suddenly, as he slowly reached for the door handle, he heard a noise from the other end of the barracks. He turned to see a pile of mattress' moving. He rushed over and started throwing them to the side and there below them was Jenna barely conscious. "Jenna, I thought I lost you," he cried as he took her in his arms. "Are you okay my love?" he asked as he held her so tight. All she could do was moan as she slowly started to regain her strength. "Come my love we must leave this place. It is no longer safe for us," he whispered as he got her to her feet. "We must get to the village. There is a safe house waiting there for us," as he helped her to the door. At the door they stopped and he looked at her and asked, "Are you ready my love?"

She looked at him with glassy eyes and quietly whispered, "Yes my love," as they took each other in their arms.

"Good," he said as he took her by the hand and opened the door and led her to the back gate. They could hear the fighting still going on behind them as they made their way through the camp and to the back gate. As they reached there they ducked behind one of the buildings. Ethan could see that there was very little opportunity to get through the gate for there was fighting going on there also. He quickly looked around to see what else they could do as out the corner of his eye he could see a small hole in the fence. Quickly he pulled her to her feet and made his way to the hole with her close behind. As soon as they got to the hole he did not hesitate as he made his way through it with her in tow. Once outside the fence they made their way to the woods with bullets still flying all about from both sides of the fight. Once in the woods they did not stop until they were out of range of the gunfire. There they stopped for a moment so Ethan could get a good look at Jenna. "Are you okay Jenna?" he asked as he checked her for wounds.

"I am okay my love," she responded as she tried to catch her breath from the long run.

"I thought I lost you," he cried as he took her in his arms. There for a moment they embraced into a deep loving hug. "Okay Jenna we have to go now. It is too dangerous to be out here. Americans are everywhere," he whispered as he once again took her by the hand and led the way through the woods for what felt like forever. Finally, they got to the edge of the woods and could see the village straight ahead. Jenna could feel Ethan squeeze her hand just a little bit harder as they broke through the woods and headed to the village. Ethan relieved that they were finally going to be safe took a deep breath when suddenly he could hear Americans shouting at them "Halt." Ethan turned to see a small squad of Americans coming right for them. Ethan quickly threw his arms in the air screaming in broken English, "Don't shoot," as he stepped between them and Jenna.

The soldier shouted "get on your knees."

"Please, please we need to get to the village," Ethan shouted.

Behind the soldiers was Ariana who everyone saw as the American commander who was trying to keep everything calm. "It is all okay. Just do as the Sergeant says and everything will be okay," the commander yelled in German.

The soldier again yelled for them to get to their knees and just as they did gunfire from the other side of the field rang out where a bullet hit the Sergeant right in the chest. It was the camp commander and a small squad of German soldiers. Gunfire started flying all around Ethan and Jenna catching them in a crossfire. Ethan quickly threw his body on top of Jenna's. Suddenly as fast as the gunfire started it ended. As the gunfire stopped Ethan looked up to see only the two opposing commanders standing opposite sides of the field. Everyone else from both squads was dead. Ethan still covering Jenna's body with his whispered "it is okay Jenna they are all dead. Come let's get up now" as he rouse to his feet. Ethan did not notice that he was full of blood. "Jenna," he said as he reached down to her. As he touched her he could feel the lifelessness of her. "Jenna," he said again as he fell to his knees next to her. "No," he screamed as he took her into his arms. "Please Jenna get up," he cried as he rocked back and forth with her in his arms. Gabriella as the commander just stood there gazing at Ethan in satisfaction. Off to the side the gypsies were also standing by watching it all. To everyone they looked like two villagers. "Please Jenna don't leave me," he screamed as he buried his head into her lifeless body. As he looked back up, he found himself in the area of Wounded Knee Creek in southwestern South Dakota in the late 19th-century standing next to Gabriella who everyone saw as Daniel F. Royer. He could hear Royer say what an uncivilized Godforsaken culture these savages are as they watched the Lakota Indians do their "Ghost Dance." Royer disgusted with it all looked at Ethan and the other soldiers and said "go over there and break up that disrespectful dancing." The other soldiers quickly started heading toward the Dancers yelling to stop. Ethan tagged a little behind them as he really did not see anything wrong with the dancing. The Dancers started pushing back on the approaching soldiers where a struggle ensued. The soldiers started hitting the unarmed Dancers with their weapons causing the tribe to start running in fear. As they did one of the females who was standing off to the side got knocked down. Ethan seeing how she could not get back up with everyone running around her headed over to her and reached down and grabbed her hand to help her up. As he took her hand she looked up and their eyes connected. Instantly they both got locked in the moment of deep feelings of love. Ethan then pulled her up and for a moment they stood there gazing into each other when suddenly one of the other soldiers broke it up telling her to get out of the area. She quickly turned to run off but Ethan held her hand and asked "wait what is your name?"

"Jenna," she replied as the soldier again screamed for her to leave. Ethan then let go of her hand as she ran off as he just stood there gazing at her.

Royer was not satisfied with just breaking up the dancing. He had just taking over as the head of the Pine Ridge Agency and was both displeased with and fearful of their religion. Royer was convinced that the Ghost Dancers were militant and threatened to destroy the U.S. government's decades-long effort to "civilize" the Lakota. By the time of his appointment many of the Lakota tribe had become passionate Dancers who incorporating white "ghost shirts" painted with various symbols that they believed would protect them from bullets. Because of this when the Bureau of Indian Affairs requested a list of Indian "troublemakers" to be slated for relocation; Royer placed influential Dancers at the top of his list and demanded that the military address the matter. In the meantime, Royer ordered Ethan and a few other soldiers to stand guard over the tribe. The soldiers set up a small camp area right outside of the Indian reservation. They would then take turns standing guard over the tribe. Every chance Ethan got he would make his way to Jenna who was on the other side of the reservation. Ethan and Jenna would then make their way outside of the reservation where they would walk hand-in-hand for hours. They would often walk until they could not hear the noise of the reservation. There they would be alone together in the silence of their love for each other under the wide-open starry sky of the Great Plains. This went on for months with Jenna and Ethan falling deeper into a true love for each other. However, as the moments fell into the past tensions started to rise between the Lakota tribe and the soldiers. Both Jenna and Ethan began to worry as the tribe got restless from being so confined. To make matters worse, the 7th Cavalry, commanded by Col. James W. Forsyth, had arrived as Royer had asked for. This was the largest deployment of federal troops since the end of the Civil War in 1865. Immediately they took over guarding the reservation where tensions rapidly escalated from the bad blood between the 7th Cavalry and the tribes because of the victory of the Lakota and Northern Cheyenne over the late Gen. George Armstrong Custer and the 7th Cavalry at Little Bighorn. Col. Forsyth quickly decreed that the Ghost Dancing was an act of terrorism and must immediately cease. Among the tribes lived Sitting Bull, a powerful Hunkpapa Lakota chief and spiritual leader who had led the Lakota and Northern Cheyenne to victory at the Little Bighorn. Many of his 250 followers were Dancers, and, though he personally was not a practitioner, he refused to let the federal government repress them any further. The Cavalry Commanders resolved to arrest Sitting

Bull for his role in permitting the spread of the Ghost Dance religion then commanded U.S. Army forces onto the Lakota lands. Sitting Bull was compliant, but his followers would not relinquish him without protest. A vicious struggle ensued, and nine Hunkpapa were killed; among the dead was Sitting Bull. The death of Sitting Bull struck fear into the hearts of those Lakota who had been opposed to reservation life. Some, numbering in the thousands, gathered in the Stronghold region of the South Dakota Badlands in preparation for a U.S. attack. As Ethan heard of the struggle he rushed to the reservation. His heart was pounding the whole way in fear that something happened to Jenna. How could he live without her is all he could think as he drove his horse faster and faster. As he arrived he started asking the remaining Indians "What happened? Where is everyone?"

"They killed Sitting Bull and took his body away," some of the remaining Indians expressed.

"Where is the rest of the tribe?" as he anxiously looked around.

"They all left to find safety in the Badlands," one of the Indians replied.

Ethan quickly got back on his horse and headed there. He just about rode his horse to death as he pushed it to go faster and faster. After a long while of steadily riding he could see up ahead the tribe heading into the Badlands. As he caught up to them, he in a state of panic started searching through the thousands of Indians to find Jenna. "Have you seen Jenna?" he would ask a few of them and they just shock their tired head no. Deeper he went into the tribe looking for her. Again he asked a few more Indians "Have you seen Jenna?" where again the despondent Indians just shock their head no. Ethan could feel the heaviness of the sadness as he continued searching when from behind him he heard a voice.

"She is not here," one of the squaws barely spoke.

"Where is she?" he asked as he headed for her.

"She went with the others."

"To where, with who?"

"She is with Big Foot and some of the others. They are going to Pine Ridge."

"Why?"

"They want to be with Red Cloud. They hope they can end the bloodshed," the squaw said with tears in her eyes.

Quickly Ethan turned his horse around and headed to Pine Ridge.

As Ethan made his way to them he could feel his horse giving in to the hard ride but he did not let up a bit as all he could think about was getting to Jenna.

Meanwhile the rest of the tribe including Jenna were rushing to Pine Ridge, where the Oglala chief Red Cloud was attempting to negotiate the preservation of Lakota traditions without bloodshed. Miniconjou Lakota chief Sitanka, known to the white Americans as Big Foot, hoped to join those at Pine Ridge to help find a peaceful resolution to this tense matter. Although he was not a Ghost Dancer he had been placed on the BIA's list of hostiles. As he was leading some 350 Miniconjou southwest from the Cheyenne River reservation to Pine Ridge reservation, the U.S. Army grew fearful of his intentions. The Cavalry Commanders ordered a detachment of the 7th Cavalry to intercept Big Foot, confiscate all weapons in his band, and escort them to a military prison at Fort Omaha, Nebraska. The detachment, commanded by Col. James W. Forsyth, reached the Miniconjou's near Wounded Knee Creek, located roughly 20 miles northeast of the Pine Ridge Agency. Big Foot saw Forsyth's scouts and informed them that he would surrender without resistance. Col. Forsyth convened with the Miniconjou's to begin the process of weapons confiscation. He herded them into a nearby clearing, had their men form a council circle, and surrounded the circle with his soldiers. He also positioned four Hotchkiss guns on a hilltop bordering the clearing. Col. Forsyth was clear in his terms: the Miniconjou must surrender all their weapons. Big Foot was hesitant, but he surrendered a few guns as a token of peace. Forsyth was not satisfied and ordered a complete search of the people and their camp, where his men discovered a host of hidden weapons. The increasingly intrusive search angered some of the Miniconjou. A man named Sits Straight began to dance the Ghost Dance and attempted to rouse the other members of the band, claiming that bullets would not touch them if they donned their sacred ghost shirts. The soldiers grew tense as Sits Straight's dance reached a frenzy. At this time Ariana arrived in hope to find a peaceful resolution that everyone saw as Maj. James McLaughlin, the reservation's agent. Immediately the Major started yelling for everyone to calm down but when a deaf Miniconjou named Black Coyote refused to give up his gun, the weapon accidentally went off, and the fraught situation turned violent as the detachment opened fire. Because many of the Miniconjou had already given up their weapons, they were left defenseless. Scores of Miniconjou were shot and killed in the first few moments, among them Big Foot. Ethan finally reaching the site could see what was going on. He could feel his heart pounding harder than ever before as he could see the Indians being massacred. As he jumped from his horse screaming for them to stop the shooting but to no avail when out the side of his eye he saw that some women and children along with Jenna attempted to flee the scene seeking protection in a nearby ravine. Ethan screamed to Jenna to get down as he started running to her. Jenna could not hear Ethan looked up and started running to him. Ethan continued to scream for her to get down as she steadily ran to Ethan when suddenly Ethan heard the horrible sound of the Hotchkiss guns as the mounted soldiers started firing on their position cutting the children, women and Jenna down. Ethan could feel his heart throb in pain as he watched the bullets ripped through Jenna. As Ethan reached her lifeless body he fell to his knees and took her into his arms. All he could do was sob and scream for her to come back. Through the whole massacre Royer stood watching from afar. Off to the far side of the massacre stood Ariana and further across the field stood the gypsies, who everyone saw as two settlers, watched it all. Ethan continued to uncontrollably sob where as he lifted his head with tears in his eyes he found himself in slave ridden Kentucky of 1850 America. There Ethan found himself as the son of a brutal slave owner who in reality was Gabriella.

"Get out of the wagon," he could hear his father yell as he stopped his horse drawn wagon. Ethan could see the fear in the faces of the slaves as his father climbed into the wagon with his whip in hand and kicked and punched at them as they tried so hard to safely get down from the wagon. One by one they jumped and fell from the wagon and coward into a group off to the side of the wagon. As the father threw the last one from the wagon he jumped down and started whipping at the group to move toward the little shack off to the side of the barn. Ethan could hear the cries of pain from a few of the slaves as his father forced then right pass Ethan and to the shack. Suddenly the father's whip hit the biggest of the group who yelled out and leaped in pain knocking over one of the women slaves who fell right next to Ethan. The father quickly started yelling at her "get up you lazy nigger bitch." The slave tried to get up but Ethan could see that she was having difficulty in doing so because of the chains that bound her. "Ethan's father yelled again "get up you filthy nigger," as he started heading straight for her. Ethan feeling sorry for her gently reached down and helped her to her feet. As she stood she thankfully looked up into Ethan's eyes where instantly Ethan could feel the deep soul penetrating love for her. By this time Ethan's father made his way to her yanking her from Ethan's hands yelling "get with the rest nigger," as he tossed her into the group. He then continued pushing them into the shack as Ethan stood there gazing at the woman as she faded from view into the shack. Ethan just stood there is a daze staring at the shack for what felt like forever until his father suddenly grabbed him yelling, "What did I tell you about touching those niggers? They are impure dirty filthy animals. God only knows what you might catch from them. Just get into the house boy," as he tossed him in the direction of the house. The next morning Ethan rose early and made his way straight outside. He knew his father got up early to get the slaves into the fields. All he wanted was to just catch a glimpse of the woman for she was all he could think about all night long. As he got outside there was no sign of his father or the slaves. With his heart still pounded in deep feelings for her he made his way to the shack and looked through the window. The shack was empty except for the make shift beds lying about the floor. He could see how the slaves had to sleep practically on top of each other in the tiny shack. He then turned and headed to the cotton fields where he knew his father would have taking them. His father's plantation was the largest in the county which took a lot of help and time to farm. He would take the slaves out early in the morning and stay well into the dark. He would literally work the slaves to death and just go get some more as needed of which there never seem to be a shortage of. At last count he had at least 20 slaves with at least 5 times going to get more. However, all Ethan could think about was just one slave; the woman who has touched his soul. As he made his way through the plantation to the crop he could feel his heart pound harder and harder so much from the excitement of wanting to see her that it took his breath away. As he arrived, he could see his father standing on the wagon with a bullwhip in his hand as he looked over the slaves picking the cotton. Ethan stood on the edge of the field for a short while combing over the sight of the workers in hope to spot her. The crop spread out for miles which made it hard to see everyone. After a few minutes Ethan started to give up hope at seeing her when out the side of his eye there she was filling a bale. For a moment she stood up and their eyes locked onto each other. Ethan could feel the passion of want of her rush through his entire being. There they stood gazing into each other's soul. For a brief moment it felt like forever to them where there was no one and nothing else. There was just them two locked within the energy of love. Suddenly the father yelled "get back to work you piece of shit nigger" as he snapped the bullwhip at her. This scared Ethan to death as he almost jumped out of his skin. He could feel his heart pounding harder than it ever had before as their gaze broke and he looked at his father standing there as angry as always. Again he yelled, "You all better get back to work or I will whip you all until there is nothing left to your nigger skin." Ethan could feel his disgust to how his father treated these people. He truly had a good heart and was nothing like his father. He felt shame for the way his father was and how he treated others and thought how one day he would help these poor people as he looked back at Jenna who was once again working as hard as she could. Ethan spent the whole day just hanging out close enough to see Jenna but far enough away that it did not cause any more problems with his father. As the sun began to set his mother called out to him that super was ready and that he should come now. "Wait mom a little longer," he yelled back.

"No come now. It is going to get cold," she yelled back.

"Please mom, just a little longer," he yelled again.

"Stop giving your mother a hard time and get into the house boy," Ethan heard his father yell.

Ethan turned to look at where the voice was coming from and there was his father standing right behind him.

"Get into the house now boy," his father yelled again.

Ethan then started heading to the house while out the side of his eye watched Jenna as she kept on working in the field. His father then turned and walked back to the slaves. His father never ate with them when he was doing the harvest. He worked the slaves until it was too dark to see. He did not want to waste a moment of sunlight and worked the slaves as hard as he could without even giving them a break. He would just have one of the slaves take water and some bread to the others but they were not allowed to stop working as they ate and drank. They had to quickly take a bite and a drink and continue with what they were doing. As Ethan got to the house his mother said, "Go wash up and then come help me with pouring the drinks for dinner." Ethan went over to the water pump and washed up. He then slowly walked back to the house so he could see Jenna one last time before he settled down for the night. As he, his mother and his three brothers and one sister ate Ethan asked his mother, "Why does he act the way he does? Why does he treat people the way he does?"

"Your father had a rough life. He had to work hard since a child and thinks everyone is not as good as him because he did," his mother replied.

"Just because someone has to work hard in their life does not give them the right to be so brutal to everyone else. He should try to help them more then hurt them," Ethan said with a tone of anger and compassion in his voice.

"He is a good man your father. He just does not know how to show it."

Ethan just dismissed her comments and continued with eating his dinner in disapproval. Later that night his father came in and immediately started complaining about the new slaves. "Those lazy niggers did not get half of what I wanted done today. I can already see that I am going to have to whip the flesh from them to get them moving," he angrily said as he sat down at the dinner table. It actually seemed like he derived pleasure from whipping the slaves more than trying to get them to work harder. Through the whole diner and night all he did was drink and complain where with each word each drink he would just get angrier. Ethan could not stand the way he spoke about the people. Every other word was nigger this and nigger that. Just such overwhelming negative expression in every way he could express it. After a while Ethan just could not take it anymore and left the room to his bedroom where he fell fast asleep dreaming of Jenna. The next day Ethan could hear his father was up bright and early. Ethan could tell he was still angry by the sound of his heavy walk toward the front door. Ethan worried about what his father would do quickly jumped out of bed, got dressed and headed out the door right behind him. He was worried that his father would hurt the slaves and wanted to make sure he tried to stop him if he did. As he got outside his father was already at the slave shack yelling and screaming for them to get up and get ready for work. For no good reason he started whipping at them in the house. Ethan could hear them screaming and his father yelling "shut up you stupid niggers and get outside and go to work". As he watched each slave run from the house trying to get dressed as they ran his heart fell deeper into his soul as he could not see Jenna. All of a sudden there she was being dragged by his father and tossed into the dirt as he yelled "I said hurry the fuck up you ignorant nigger" as he whipped her. Jenna screamed in pain as she tried to get to her feet as the father whipped at her again hitting square on her back. She screamed as she fell to the ground as Ethan could see the blood pour through her shirt as he headed to her to help her up. The father yelled at Ethan "back off boy," stopping him in his tracks as his father started toward her as she squirmed in pain trying to get back to her feet as the father started kicking and swearing at her. Finally she got to her feet and ran to join the rest of the slaves who were cowering by the wagon. Ethan felt so helpless that he could not do anything for them. The father got them all into the wagon and drove off to the fields. Ethan just stood there with his heart aching for Jenna as they drove out of sight. Ethan just knew that this all was just going to get worse as he headed to the barn to do his chores. All he could think about was how his father was going to continue to beat them and treat them horribly for as long as they were under his control as he finished up his chores. He then headed to the house to get something to drink pondering what he was going to do to free Jenna from this horrid existence. Over the next few months Ethan and Jenna fell deeper into feelings of love for each other. Each night Ethan would wait for his father to drink himself into an unconscious sleep and then grab the key to the shack lock and then sneak out to the shack to meet Jenna. Jenna would be waiting for him right inside the door and as he unlocked the lock they would go off hand-in-hand together to their secret spot on the edge of the tree line under the stars. There they felt like they were so alone in the world far away from all of the pain and suffering. Most nights they would just sit in silence with Jenna snuggled into Ethan's caring embrace. Other nights they would talk about somehow getting away from the abuse of the father who over the months had gotten more abusive to all of the slaves. This went on until one night while the father was slowly drinking himself to sleep he heard a noise. He jumped up grabbed the key while bitching about the niggers trying to escape as he headed to the front door. Ethan quickly said, "It was just the wind father," as he tried so hard to calm him down and get him back to the table.

"No, I know it is those fucking niggers trying to escape," his father bellowed as he rushed out the door.

"No father, please come back inside," Ethan cried as he followed his father out the door and to the shack.

As they got to the shack his father quickly unlocked the lock and threw open the door and there was Jenna happily waiting for her love.

"I knew it," his father screamed as he pulled Jenna from the shack. "You filthy little nigger, you were trying to escape weren't you," he yelled as he threw her to the ground. "I will teach you to disobey me," he continued yelling as he headed to the barn to get his whip.

"No father, she was not trying to escape. Please father don't," Ethan cried as his father just ignored him and continued to the barn. Ethan then turned to Jenna and told her to run as he then turned and headed to the barn. Jenna scared to death to do anything cried out Ethan's name as she found the strength to get to her feet. Ethan for a split second turned to her where their eyes connected as Ethan cried, "Run to our secret spot Jenna." With tears in her eyes Jenna turned and ran. Ethan then turned back to barn and just as he got there his father had grabbed his whip and was heading back out the door. Ethan quickly got in front of him and screamed "No father she was just standing at the door. It is all okay. Let's go back inside the house."

"No boy, I must teach those niggers a lesson," the father screamed as he pushed Ethan aside. Ethan quickly got back in front of his father screaming "No father," as his father backed handed him to the face knocking him out as he fell to the ground. It was daybreak when Ethan started to regain consciousness. Through a daze he could hear the hound dogs howling and a crowd of angry men screaming that they must find her. Ethan overcoming his dizziness got to his feet and ran out of the barn to see the angry crowd of men heading in the wrong direction. Ethan quickly started running toward where he knew Jenna was waiting. As he got there Jenna was nowhere in sight. He quietly called out to her but for a moment nothing and then with fear in her face she stepped out from behind the big oak tree. As soon as they saw each other they ran into each other's arms where Jenna nearly collapsed from exhausting and fear. "I got you Jenna. All is going to be okay now. I will keep you safe," he said as he held her tight. Suddenly they heard the hound dogs howling in the distance. "We have to go now Jenna," Ethan said as he grabbed her hand and they started running as fast as they could. They ran throughout the day and into the night. As the full moon set high in the sky and they could no longer hear the hound dogs they stopped to rest awhile. They both remained silent as Ethan took her into his arms and they fell together against the tree exhausted. There they remained throughout the rest of the night with Jenna feeling safe within Ethan's embrace. As the new day broke, Ethan looked down into Jenna's face as she rested in his arms. He then kissed her softly on her forehead and she moaned in safe pleasure as she fell deeper into his embrace. Slowly she woke to Ethan's words "I love you Jenna," as she whispered back "I love you Ethan." For a moment they sat there holding each other tight. Jenna then asked, "What are we going to do Ethan?"

Ethan hesitated for a moment and then said, "There is a man named Levi Coffin who lives just across the river in Ohio. I heard he helps slaves escape to their freedom through what is called an "underground railroad". I know some folks close to here that can help us get in contact with him so he can help us".

Jenna looked worried about this and asked, "Is it safe? What about you?"

"As far as I hear, yes it is. I will stay here and make sure no one comes after you."

"But I do not want to go without you," she cried.

"It will be all okay. I will come to you as soon as I can and then we can live the life we dreamed about. Now let's go and make sure you act like my slave in case we pass anyone. We do not want anyone getting suspicious". This made her feel a little better as they started out. They tried the best they could to not come across anyone as the made their way down the dirt road. Whenever they did Ethan would treat her like a slave which he really did not like doing. As they got a couple miles down the road Ethan took them into the woods where they could see a little farm house. "You stay here for a moment while I go speak to them," Ethan whispered to Jenna.

"No Ethan. I am afraid," she whispered back.

"Do not worry you will be able to see me. I will be right over there at that barn," as he pointed it out to her. "Just stay right here and I will be back as fast as I can," as he sat her down by the big tree and headed off to the barn. Jenna sat quietly worried as she watched Ethan make his way to the barn. Just as he got there a man carrying a shotgun walked out of the barn. She could see that they knew each other as they shook hands. For what seemed like forever they stood there talking as Jenna worriedly watched. Ethan than turned and started walking back to her as the man started walking to the farm house. She could see Ethan walking really fast which made her feel at ease. As he reached her he took her into his arms. For a moment they just embraced each other without a word. As Ethan slowly let her go and took her by the hands he said, "We are in luck my dear sweet Jenna.

My friend James said that Levi was coming tonight to bring as many slaves as possible safely across the river to their freedom and you can go with him. All we have to do is wait here until it gets dark and he will signal us when it is time for us to come," Ethan said as they quietly sat in each other's arms by the tree. They did not speak a word as the darkness of the night slowly took over the day. Ethan could feel Jenna nervously shake as they sat there in the pitch black of a moonless night waiting for the signal. Ethan pulled her tight to help ease her fear as they just sat there staring at the barn. Suddenly they could see the light of a lantern swinging through the darkness. Ethan quickly jumped up as he said, "there it is, time to go Jenna," as he pulled her to her feet. There was not even a moment to think as they rushed through the woods and to the light. As they got to the light there was James. "Over there," he said as he pointed to the other side of the barn at a group slaves huddled by the glow of another lantern. Ethan quickly rushed her to them. When they got there they could see the fear in the eyes of the men, women and children. Ethan then sat Jenna down within the group and said "Wait here Jenna. Everything is okay now. You are going to be free soon." Jenna nervously sat down within the group as Ethan let go of her hand as he turned and went back to James. Just as he reached him he heard behind him the sound of a horse drawn wagon coming down the dirt road. He turned to see two horses slowly pulling a large topless flatbed wagon with Ariana, who Ethan saw as a man, sitting atop a high raised bench seat at the reins with another man sitting next to him. The man carefully pulled the wagon close to the group of people and got down from his seat. Ethan turned to James and asked, "Is that him?"

"Yes, that is the President of the Underground Railroad himself, Levi Coffin," James answered as Levi quickly had one of the man slaves from the group get up on the wagon as the other man who was with Levi now held the reins. Levi then turned back to the group and had the rest of the men slaves help gather and escort the women and children to the wagon. Ethan watched as Jenna moved along with the group to the side of the wagon. Once there Jenna turned to Ethan with love tears in her eyes and whispered "I love you Ethan" as she turned to get onto the wagon when suddenly from behind the wagon Ethan's father and a group of men in white hoods burst through the tree line screaming, "There you are you nigger whore. Thought you could get away from me didn't you you filthy nigger," as he and the group of men started shooting randomly into the group of slaves. One of the first bullets hit the slave who was standing on the wagon helping others to get on the wagon. This slave fell on top of Jenna. In the chaos of it all the man holding the reins jumped down and quickly shielded and escorted Levi to safety.

"Oh my God," Ethan screamed as both he and James started running towards the group. "Stop father stop," Ethan cried out as the father just kept pulling the trigger of his rifle while screaming "Die you filthy niggers." One after the other the bullets found their random targets as one slave after the other fell dead.

"Jenna," Ethan screamed as she tried to get from beneath the dead body of the slave. Ethan could see her struggling to lift the body from her but as hard as she could she just could not lift the heavy body of the man off of her as she screamed out to Ethan, "Help Ethan, please help", as she continued to try to lift the body from her. Suddenly she gasped for breath as she looked up and there was the father standing above her with his rifle pointing at her. "Die you filthy nigger whore," he said as he pulled the trigger and shot her right through the heart.

"No," Ethan screamed as he fell to his knees in tearful grief beside her lifeless body.

Off to the side of it all Levi helpless watched the horror of it all. Also off to the side were the gypsies, who everyone saw as the teenage children of James. As they stood there watching, the grey witch Soleena appeared right behind them. "Did you get to see what you needed to see Mukesh?" Soleena asked.

The man looked at the girl and asked, "Do you see what I mean?"

"Yes," she replied

"Then it is time to stop this?" Soleena said.

"Yes," Muhesh said as Soleena appeared behind Gabriella.

"Enough Gabriella," Soleena said.

Startled, Gabriella turned and saw it was Soleena and screamed "Never will I let go;" just as Soleena reached out and touched Gabriella's heart saying "May all be as it should be."

Suddenly there was Ethan and Jenna once again doing crash baby with Jenna falling but this time Ethan grabbing her by the arm and pulling her safely back to his side as the car flew by. "Oh my God Jenna, that was so close. Thank God I caught you in time. I would have suffered for eternity if you had died," Ethan said as he moved her to his other side away from the street. "There, you walk on this side of me from now on away from danger," Ethan whispered as he kissed her on the cheek as they continued to walk hand-in-hand within their love for each other.

At the very same moment Gabriella appeared in the rocking chair by the fireplace in the witch house in the woods. There she sat rocking deep in thought of it all as her hair slowly started turning grey.

OTHER ANAPHORA LITERARY PRESS TITLES

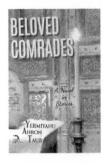

Beloved Combrades
By: Yermiyahu Ahron Taub

Notes for Further Research
By: Molly Kirschner

Falling and Other Stories
By: Ben Stoltzfus

The Visit
By: Michael G. Casey

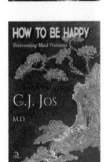

How to Be Happy
By: C. J. Jos

A Dying Breed
By: Scott Duff

Love in the Cretaceous
By: Howard W. Robertson

Emergence: The Role of Mindfulness in Creativity
By: Rosie Rosenzweig

Lightning Source UK Ltd.
Milton Keynes UK
UKHW010251270721
387818UK00001B/18